Rabbit Goes Duck Hunting

Rabbit Goes Duck Hunting

A Traditional Cherokee Legend

A GRANDMOTHER STORY

Story by Deborah L. Duvall

Drawings by Murv Jacob

University of New Mexico Press
Albuquerque

Dedication

Dr. Bill Wiggins and Teresa "Muffie" Miller

©2004 by the University of New Mexico Press
Text © 2004 by Deborah L. Duvall
Illustrations © 2004 by Murv Jacob
First edition
All rights reserved.

Library of Congress Cataloging-in-Publication Data

Duvall, Deborah L., 1952–
Rabbit goes duck hunting : a traditional Cherokee legend /
drawings by Murv Jacob ; story by Deborah L. Duvall.— 1st ed.
p. cm. — (Grandmother stories ; v. 5)
ISBN 0-8263-3336-2 (cloth : alk. paper)
1. Cherokee Indians—Folklore. I. Jacob, Murv, ill. II. Title.
E99.C5D895 2005
398.24'52932'08997557—dc22
2004005282

Design by Melissa Tandysh
Printed and bound in Singapore by C.S. Graphics Pte. Ltd.

Rabbit, whose name is Ji-Stu,
awoke one morning to the warm, summer
sun of the Smoky Mountains, shining through
his front door and onto his face.

He stepped outside his house into the broom grass meadow and looked at the sky. There was nothing but blue as far as he could see.

"Today is a good day to travel," Ji-Stu said to himself. "Maybe I'll go up the river and visit Otter. I can be there by noon if I hurry."

Ji-Stu gathered up his cooking pot and spoon, his best blanket
and some dried corn and beans. These he rolled into a pack that he
carried on his shoulder. Within minutes, he was off. Ji-Stu stayed close
by the river as he traveled. He knew that Otter spent sunny days like
this swimming and fishing. Otter could be anywhere.

Before long, Ji-Stu came upon a wide bend in the river. The water near the gravel bar was calm, and floating upon it were hundreds of wood ducks. They sat in a big circle, all facing the center. Ji-Stu threw down his pack and ran to the gravel bar to get a closer look at the huge creature who rose in the middle. In all his travels, Ji-Stu had never seen a wood duck to match the size of this one.

"Surely I am looking at the Chief of All the Wood Ducks," Ji-Stu chuckled aloud. "Just wait until Otter hears about this!"

Ji-Stu remembered hearing Otter talk about the great Wood Duck. Otter bragged and bragged that one day he would see the old Chief. Now Ji-Stu the Rabbit bounded down the path faster than ever, looking for Otter and grinning from ear to ear. It was his turn to brag!

Ji-Stu did not have to wait long. The river bank deepened as he neared a clear spring that fell several feet to the river below. There Otter stood, beneath the spring, feasting on the shiny minnows he spied inside the waterfall.

Otter and Ji-Stu saw each other at the same moment. Now everyone knows that Ji-Stu is the Trickster of all the animals, and Otter knew this better than most. Ji-Stu had tricked him more than once. But Otter liked Ji-Stu just the same. He told the most interesting stories, and Otter liked stories better than anything.

He waved and said, "Si-yo, Ji-Stu, hello! What are you doing so far up the river?"

"I came to visit you, Otter," Ji-Stu said, and then he began to sing. "I have seen the greatest thing, and this I will not tell you, this I will not tell you."

Otter's eyes lit up. One thing he knew for sure. Ji-Stu could not keep from telling a secret, no matter how hard he tried. Otter would have his story any moment now.

"I've seen someone you would like to know!" Ji-Stu teased again.

Otter leaned back against a hickory tree and yawned. He even pretended to go to sleep as Ji-Stu got more and more excited.

"Someone you would like to know and someone you have never seen," Ji-Stu chanted as he circled around Otter. "And he is the Chief of All the ..."

"Wood Ducks!" Otter snorted. "You are joking, Ji-Stu. The Chief of all the Wood Ducks never comes to this river. I would certainly have seen him."

"Come with me and I will show you," Ji-Stu laughed, jumping up and down. "I saw him myself just down the river a ways. All the wood ducks are there, sitting in a circle around him, and he is twice the size of Eagle!"

Of course Otter knew better than to believe Ji-Stu, but he loved the taste of wood ducks. Maybe he really would see hundreds of them

together, and he would have a fine feast! Otter followed happily along as
Ji-Stu led the way.

Ji-Stu and Otter moved quietly through the river cane along the edge
of the gravel bar. Otter had never seen so many ducks! But the great
Chief of All the Wood Ducks was nowhere in sight.

For once, Ji-Stu had nothing to say. But Otter did not even ask about the Chief. He slipped into the river, winked at Ji-Stu and disappeared. As Ji-Stu looked after him, he saw a wood duck vanish into the water. Otter had caught his duck, and none of the other ducks even noticed.

Ji-Stu thought about this for a moment. "If Otter can catch a duck, then I can too. But I will catch a bigger duck!"

He pulled a green grapevine down from a tree and shaped it into a noose. Then he dived under the water and opened his eyes. All around him were webbed feet, paddling in the water. Just then, he saw two huge yellow feet plunge down right before his eyes. The Chief of All the Wood Ducks was back, and he sat on the water just above Ji-Stu!

Ji-Stu popped his head up behind the big duck and silently slipped the noose around the Chief's neck. He pulled as hard as he could, but nothing happened. When he pulled again, the Chief turned to see Ji-Stu bobbing in the water. With a loud quack, he swam deep down to the bottom of the river, as Ji-Stu held fast to the grapevine noose.

The flock of ducks took off flapping and squawking in every direction as the Chief of All the Wood Ducks dragged Ji-Stu back to the surface. Then he spread his powerful wings and began to fly, yanking Ji-Stu into the air behind him.

"Let go, Ji-Stu!" yelled Otter from the gravel bar. "You don't even eat ducks!"

But Otter quickly became a tiny thing standing far below. He could only watch as his old friend disappeared over the treetops.

Afraid to hang on and afraid to let go, Ji-Stu thought about the trouble he was in, and how stupid he must look to anyone on the ground below. Maybe he would get lucky and no one would see him. How silly he had been! His only reason for trying to catch the big duck was to show off for Otter, and now he was really in a fix.

Suddenly Ji-Stu heard laughter and shouting from below. Through the trees he glimpsed the cooking fires and houses of a village.

"Oh, I hope no one looks up," Ji-Stu muttered to himself.

The laughter grew louder and the Chief of All the Wood Ducks flew right toward the sound. It seemed he wanted the people in the village to see the foolish Ji-Stu. What Ji-Stu saw next set his heart to pounding. Two boys ran into a clearing and both of them held a bow and arrow.

The boys had never seen such an unbelievable sight. Above them flew the biggest wood duck in the world and hanging from its neck was a full-grown rabbit. What a supper they would have tonight!

One little boy positioned his arrow on the bowstring and pulled back as hard as he could. Luckily for Ji-Stu, he was slow and clumsy with the weapon. By the time the arrow whizzed between Ji-Stu's feet, the Chief of all the Wood Ducks had flown past the clearing and out of the boy's aim.

The Chief showed no sign of landing anytime soon, and Ji-Stu was quickly losing the strength to hold on. Somehow he must get his feet back on solid ground. Maybe he could land on a tree branch and climb down. He spotted a big tree ahead, took a deep breath, and let go!

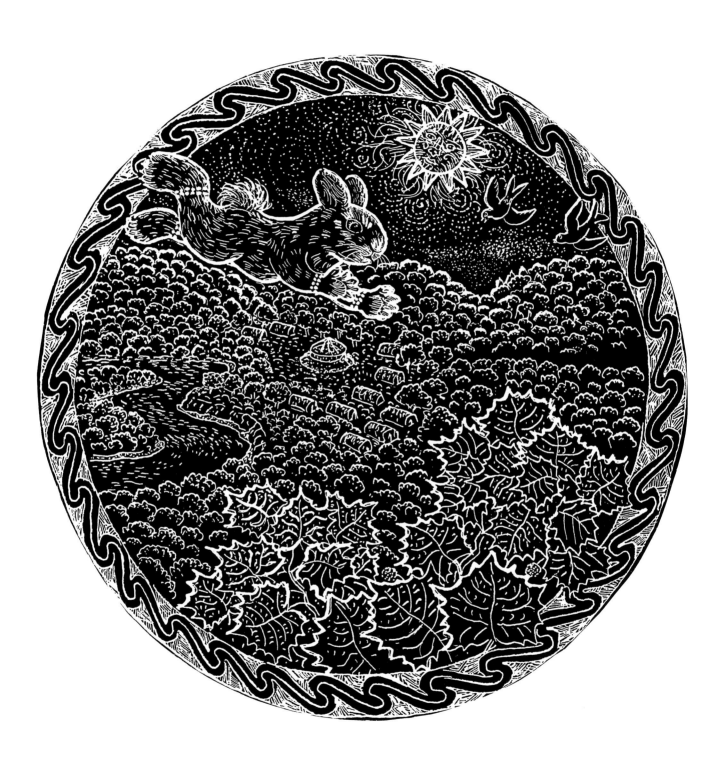

For a few seconds, Ji-Stu was surrounded by blue sky, but then he found himself falling into darkness until his feet hit something hard. He had landed deep down at the bottom of a hollow tree. Shining through a knothole in the side of the tree was the only light Ji-Stu could see.

Poor Ji-Stu was so tired he went right to sleep inside the tree. He slept on through the night and awoke only when the light came through the knothole again. It seemed safe to leave then, but try as he might Ji-Stu could not climb or jump high enough to reach the top of the tree. He longed for his snug little house and breakfast, and wondered how he would ever get home.

Just then Ji-Stu heard a rustling sound, followed by laughter. Peeking through the knothole, he saw a frightful sight. Those same two little boys from the village were just outside. Ji-Stu watched as they laid down their bows and arrows long enough to pick some ripe blackberries growing near the hollow tree. Then he had an idea.

Through the knothole in the hollow tree, Ji-Stu began to sing as loudly as he could.

"I am as pretty as I can be, I am as pretty as I can be, chop a hole and you will see!"

The boys rushed over to Ji-Stu's tree and peered through the knothole into the darkness. They tried to reach their little hands into the knothole. Ji-Stu did not make a sound until they backed away.

"Chop a hole and you will see!" Ji-Stu sang again.

The boys forgot the berries and their bows. They ran as fast as they could go to the village and each returned with a stone axe. The boys chopped away at the hollow tree. Ji-Stu made no sound until he knew the hole was big enough.

"Now look at me!" Ji-Stu yelled, and he jumped out through the hole and ran straight for the forest.

Before the little boys could grab their bows and arrows, Ji-Stu the Rabbit was out of sight.

Ji-Stu hurried away from the people's village and toward the river. There he found his pack with his fine blanket and cooking tools leaned neatly against a tree.

"Otter," he thought, smiling.

He picked up his pack and hurried down the path to the broom grass meadow and home. He could see smoke from a cooking fire in front of his house, and he could smell his favorite bean soup. Around the fire sat his good friends, Yona the Bear, Possum and, of course, Otter.

"Ji-Stu!" Otter jumped up to greet him. "We all came to hear the story of how you caught the Chief of All the Wood Ducks."

Ji-Stu only grinned.

"And we went to look for you, too, all the way to the people's village. There are two mean little boys there who shoot arrows at everyone they see!"

"I know," said Ji-stu, shaking his head. "I know."

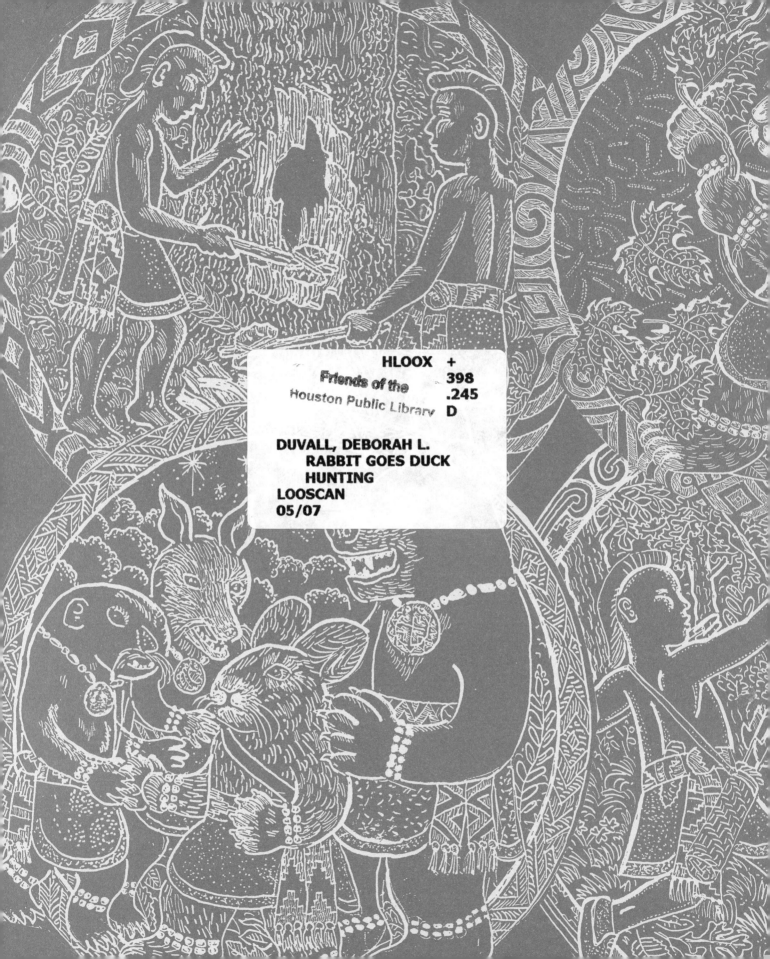